What Did I Look Like When I Was A Baby?

For Aric – T.R
For Christopher and Kate Willis – J.W

What Did I Look Like When I Was A Baby?

words by Jeanne Willis
with pictures by Tony Ross
and music by Christopher Willis . . .

Andersen Press
London

The Bullfrog Song Music © 2000 Christopher Willis
Text copyright © 2000 by Jeanne Willis. Illustration copyright © 2000 by Tony Ross
This paperback edition first published in 2003 by Andersen Press Ltd.
The rights of Jeanne Willis and Tony Ross to be identified as the author and illustrator of this work
have been asserted by them in accordance with the Copyright, Designs and Patents Act, 1988.
First published in Great Britain in 2000 by Andersen Press Ltd. 20 Vauxhall Bridge Road, London SW1V 2SA.
Published in Australia by Random House Australia Pty., 20 Alfred Street, Milsons Point, Sydney, NSW 2061.
All rights reserved. Colour separated in Italy by Fotoriproduzioni Grafiche, Verona.
Printed and bound in Italy by Grafiche AZ, Verona.

10 9 8 7 6 5

British Library Cataloguing in Publication Data available.

ISBN-10: 1 84270 210 6
ISBN-13: 978 1 84270 210 9

This book has been printed on acid-free paper

"Mum . . ." said Michael, "what did I look like when
I was a baby?"
   "You looked just like your grandad," she smiled.
"Bald and wrinkly!"

Far away in the jungle, the son of a baboon asked his mother the same question.
"Mum, what did I look like when I was a baby?"

"Pretty much the same as you do now," she said,
"only not so hairy. You were a right little monkey."

"I wonder what I looked like when I was a baby?"
thought the Hippopotamus.

"The same as you do now, only smaller," said his mother.
"Mind you, you weighed a ton even then."

"What about me, Ma?" asked the Leopard.

"You've always had spots," she said, "but your legs have grown much longer. It runs in the family."

"What did I look like when I was a baby?"
asked the Ostrich.

"You were a chick!" said her dad. "You looked just like your mum, only instead of having big bird's feathers you were all fluffy and cute."

"Mum, was I fluffy?" asked the Snake.

"Fluffy? Ssssss . . . certainly not," she hissed. "You've always had beautiful sssskin. You were a ssscaled-down version of me."

"And I've still got my rattle, Mum!" she said.

"Oi . . . Muvver! Did I look like you when I was a nipper?" asked the Hyena.

"Na!" she said. "You looked just like your dad and
we laughed and laughed and laughed!"

"What about me?" asked the Warthog. "Did I look like Father?"

"Rather!" snorted his mother. "Only he was an enormous boar."

"And me?" asked the Chameleon. "Have I always looked like this, Mum?"

"Yes," she said. "The only thing that's changed is your colour . . . Oh, there you go again!"

So, one by one, all around the world, the animals learnt
that when they were babies, they looked like little versions
of their mums and dads, pretty much. UNTIL . . .

"**Mum** . . . . ?" wondered the Bullfrog.
"Son," she said, "don't even ask!"

But the little Bullfrog went on and on and on, "Mum, what did I look like when I was a baby . . . ? What did I look like when I was a baby?" until in the end, his mother showed him a photograph.

"That's you when you were three weeks old," she said.
He stared at the photograph in horror.
"Me?" he said. "That's not me! It looks nothing like a frog!"

Angry and confused, he hid under a stone and decided never to trust his mother again.

But suddenly, he heard all his brothers and sisters singing:

Little bullfrog babies
Don't look like frogs at all,
They're small and black and slimy
And they cannot hop or crawl.
A great big head, two dots for eyes,
A mouth just like an "O",
A tadpole tail that swims behind them
Everywhere they go.
But then they grow two kicking legs,
Two tiny, webby feet,
And then two perfect, froggy arms
With fingers all complete.
Their tails shrink, they take a gulp
And climb onto a log,
And that is how a baby tadpole
Turns into a frog!

When the little bullfrog realised all the frogs in the world were once tadpoles, he felt much happier.
"I know what I looked like when I was a baby!" he smiled.

"Beautiful!" said his mother.

The Bullfrog Song

Words by Jeanne Willis

Music by Christopher Willis

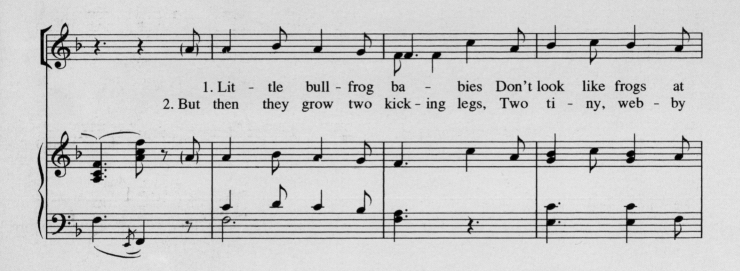

1. Lit - tle bull - frog ba - bies Don't look like frogs at
2. But then they grow two kick - ing legs, Two ti - ny, web - by

all,_____ They're small and black and sli - my And they
feet,_____ And then two per - fect, frog - gy arms With

can - not hop or crawl.__ A great big head, two dots for eyes, A
fin - gers all com - plete.__ Their tails shrink, they take a gulp And

mouth just like an 'O',____ A tad - pole tail that
climb on - to a log,____ And that is how a

swims be - hind them E - very - where they go.____
ba - by tad - pole Turns in - to a frog!__

More Andersen Press paperback picture books!

The Big Sneeze
by Ruth Brown

Betty's Not Well Today
by Gus Clarke

Dear Daddy
by Philippe Dupasquier

War and Peas
by Michael Foreman

Dilly Dally and the Nine Secrets
by Elizabeth MacDonald and Ken Brown

The Sad Story of Veronica Who Played the Violin
by David McKee

Princess Camomile Gets Her Way
by Hiawyn Oram and Susan Varley

Lazy Jack
by Tony Ross

Bear's Eggs
by Dieter and Ingrid Schubert

Rabbit's Wish
by Paul Stewart and Chris Riddell

Mr Bear and the Bear
by Frances Thomas and Ruth Brown

Frog and a Very Special Day
by Max Velthuijs

Dr Xargle's Book of Earth Hounds
by Jeanne Willis and Tony Ross